Dear Brother Alan

STEVE PRICE

for Brother Michael

PART ONE

[1]

He feels like he just opened someone else's mail
by mistake. The letter, handwritten in red on a sheet
of note paper from Smackwater Motor Inn, begins
Dear Brother Alan. He double-checks the envelope,
indeed addressed to him, Alan Fry at 22 Old Court
Lane, then reads the note, front and back. In short,
a revivalist needs him to replace the regular sinner
who has become indisposed.

Alan has a mortgage, a part-time working
spouse, one child in her second year at the most
expensive veterinary college in the country, and
another genius still in high school. He can't afford
to leave his position as Executive Vice President of
Corporate Relations at a leading provider of group
dental insurance and roam the backcountry serving
as a deterrent to amoral behavior. This Reverend

Gerald Swit must have the wrong guy. And yet something between the lines is making Alan antsy, like the time he tried pot.

"Do you have time to look at this?"

"Hold on." Regina caps the jug she just filled with water. She's about to go teach a stretching class at the senior center. She grabs the letter and starts reading.

"It doesn't have to be right now," he says, suddenly wanting it back.

She giggles as her eyes track the words.

"What's so funny?"

"This part about your predecessor!" She squeezes her thighs together to keep from urinating.

"Brother Ray? That's not funny."

"Gambling? Drinking? Idleness?"

"I don't see the humor."

"As if you have any of these qualifications! Hey Todd! Come down here and look at this kooky letter your father just got!"

"Leave him alone. He's studying for a test."

"Fine, I'll throw it out if it bothers you so much."

"It doesn't *bother* me."

"No? Go look at your face." She steps on the pedal and drops it in.

[2]

The instant the squash racquet slipped from his hand, there was nothing Gerry Switzer could do. His opponent, just having returned a drop shot, was ten feet in front of him and the thing was speeding like an arrow toward the back of the man's head and everything became clear to Gerry Switzer. He was never in control of anything. The nursery rhyme about life being a dream was right. In 1989 he won the men's cup. That was a dream he was in.

Dreams can seem very realistic while they're taking place and this one with the zooming racquet was a good example. The rival dropped to his knees and checked his scalp for blood, and that was it for Gerry Switzer. His long dream of thwacking bounceless little balls against walls was over and a new dream began. There were mountains in the distance. He started his car, put it in gear, and watched them roll toward him.

Alan can't sleep. He didn't medicate, not tonight. He's confident there's at least a 40% chance he'll have a nightmare featuring Reverend Gerald Swit and he needs to stay sharp in case he has to wake himself up. Letting dreams play out and writing them down is easy for Dr. Seahorse to say. That's what Regina calls him, she who's never seen a therapist and sleeps like a machine.

While she's snoring away he sneaks down to the kitchen to recover the letter from the trash. It's mildly damp but unsoiled. He folds it to fit perfectly in his wallet, which goes back on the counter next to his keys.

[4]

The mountains were close enough for Gerry Switzer to drive into. The narrow road he was on continued upward. A little wooden structure had a neon sign telling him to EAT HERE. It was early in the morning. He enjoyed two cheeseburgers, home fries, and a ginger ale. When he came out, a policeman was writing him a ticket. The car was parked as much in the road as off.

"In town for the revival?" the officer guessed from the out-of-state plates.

"Yes, sir." Gerry Switzer wasn't aware of a revival but it sounded good to him, and his answer got him out of the ticket. The metal citation case clicked shut; the pen was used to point.

"There's a dirt road a quarter mile up. You'll see the sign. Park in the field and the tent will be around to your left."

The aroma of warm bagels fills the conference room. Everyone is smiling. Alan has hit this one out of the park. His initiative to slash out-of-pocket costs for root canals will revolutionize the industry.

"Amazing," says the client. "Who would even imagine the deductible could actually be lower?"

Tires screech outside, followed by a crash. Alan gets up and shuts the blinds facing the freeway. "And the coverage itself is more comprehensive," he adds, then hands the baton to Skip, who goes into the details.

"WHAT WE COVER AT THE 60% TIER," the underling projects over the sirens, "OTHER PROVIDERS DON'T COVER AT ALL!" His enthusiasm makes the yelling seem natural. While everyone's captivated, Alan sneaks the letter from his wallet and goes straight to the last sentence:

> If you hope to stand any chance of escaping
> the hell in which you have placed yourself, be
> at your curb on Thursday, May 7th by 5:15 a.m.
> ready to board a white van.

[6]

Gerry Switzer was sitting in a chair under the tent when a man who looked nothing like the elderly minister whose picture was stapled to a tree walked up to the podium. The shirt was too small. Flesh bulged between the missed belt loop and the belt.

"Good morning! Here is my question! Are you good enough for God!"

A woman in the front row rose and pointed. "That's not Reverend Wilkinsen! That's Brother Ray! He's just a sinner! He can't preach!"

The man next to her looked behind him. "What happened to the police?"

"I'm going home right now and calling them!" said another man.

Gerry Switzer remained seated while the rest of the congregants headed to the parking lot and Brother Ray ran for the woods. When Brother Ray fell and clutched his ankle, Gerry Switzer got up.

"Maybe you should go," mumbles Regina, about to fall asleep.

"Excuse me?"

"You want to go, go. Be Brother Alan for a while."

"You *want* me to go?"

"Seahorse isn't helping. You've been seeing that guy since you were nine."

Alan has nothing to add. As usual, she's put it in a nutshell.

"Just go," she yawns. "We'll still be here when you get back."

Brother Ray appreciated the ride and all but he wished Gerry Switzer would stop asking what happened to Reverend Wilkinsen. The past had never been very clear to Brother Ray. The present works better for him. He could safely say the pain that had originated in his ankle was shooting all the way up his leg.

"He might've disappeared," he grunted.

"Where would he go?"

"Might be dead."

"You just said he disappeared."

"I said might've. Might've come back to the room. Might not have been moving. Might've stopped breathing." He grimaced. "I'm talking too much."

"Did you call the police?"

"I might've told the front desk."

By the time they arrived at the hospital, enough information had come out of Brother Ray for Gerry Switzer to get the picture. Reverend Wilkinsen was old with three terminal diseases. He died in a motel and then Brother Ray tried to imitate him in hopes of walking away with the collection plate.

It turned out the ankle wasn't broken. Brother Ray kept his job as sinner and Reverend Wilkinsen's position was filled by Gerry Switzer who started going by Reverend Gerald Swit. Reverend Swit's sermons, which were only about a minute long, sent Brother Ray and everyone into tearful comas of contemplation. The collections were like jackpots, then Brother Ray's leg started killing him. They X-rayed the tibia this time and found a spiral fracture.

Brother Ray wasn't young or in good health and they told him so. He was looking at six weeks in the rehabilitation wing. Reverend Swit paid what was owed so far and struck out on his own. Brother Ray didn't warn him that folks might stop showing up. As much as they might like a preacher, nobody can relate to him. The standard is too high. You need the sinner. The sinner is the mirror that reflects the warts they have on their souls, at least that's what Reverend Wilkinsen used to say. Whether any of that was true Brother Ray didn't know. Reverend Swit would have to find out for himself.

The seahorse Dr. Seahorse is painting now is blowing apart a dandelion. Passing his days this way sure beats seeing patients. The only one left is Alan Fry, who begged him to make an exception when he announced his retirement. Dr. Seahorse agreed as long as he could paint during their sessions.

The seahorses started with a dream Dr. Seahorse had about a seahorse, which he discussed on an episode of *The David Susskind Show* featuring Jacques Cousteau. The seahorse itself is a dream, a monogamous aquatic spitting image of a horse birthed by its father and capable of eating upwards of 3,000 shrimp a day with no teeth or stomach. Anything is possible with a seahorse. Dr. Seahorse's first seahorse smoked a pipe. The one sticking a flag on the moon sold for $175,000. "It's true," said David Susskind, "anything *is* possible with a seahorse."

Nobody stayed to help Reverend Swit take down the tent. His sermon was awful. Without Brother Ray, there was no one specific to address. That's what had made the messages personal, and not just for Brother Ray. Each of them felt Reverend Swit was speaking directly to them. Preaching without a sinner was like swatting a racquet at air.

Reverend Swit got everything back in the van and drove down out of the mountains. He ended up in a suburban neighborhood where he pulled over for a nap. When he opened his eyes, a man across the street was riding a mower across a lawn that looked recently mowed. Hardly any grass was being cut. On each side of the driveway were little signs prohibiting dogs from relieving themselves, and in the driveway itself a freshly washed silver sedan shined. The man's eyes, meanwhile, shined not. Reverend Swit recognized the look. It was the look of someone in a dream that was going on too long. He noted the address, 22 Old Court Lane, and the fancy F on the screen door. There was a telephone book back at the motel. The man's name wouldn't take long to find, and there was stationary to write him a letter.

[11]

Todd, standing at his bedroom window, lowers
the binoculars. It's still too dark out to see much. On
a suitcase at the end of the driveway sits Alan, who
keeps looking at his watch. Little does he know, he
wasn't the first to take the letter from the trash.
When Regina yelled for Todd to come see it and Alan
objected, Todd stopped calculating the height of a
geyser from 100 meters away looking up at an 18°
angle and caught the rest of their conversation.
Later, when they were both upstairs for the night, he
read the letter and put it back where he found it.
Then yesterday after school, Regina had something
to tell him. Extensive business trip was how she put
it. Todd stifled a grin before it overtook his face. It
was too good to be true. He needed to set his alarm
and see for himself. And now, as the van pulls up, the
red digits give him the time. Reverend Gerald Swit is
nearly four minutes late.

16

PART TWO

[1]

The pulpit goes last. It looks like it belongs in a basilica. Reverend Swit and Brother Alan lug it under the tent and set it down beside the seat of the sinner, in which Brother Alan is looking forward to sitting. The letter didn't mention unloading and assembling 300 pounds of fabric plus iron poles, 130 metal chairs, and a monstrosity of solid mahogany. And then doing it all again in reverse.

There's a lot Reverend Swit doesn't mention. After being picked up at the house this morning, Brother Alan asked where they were headed and barely got a shrug. He let some time go by, then questioned why he was contacted in the first place. This time Reverend Swit spoke.

"Behind every monkey is a monkey's behind."

That silenced Brother Alan. He kept trying to

figure out what it could mean. And then, a short while ago, he was pounding a stake into the ground and Dr. Seahorse inexplicably popped into his mind. The first thing he realized was that Dr. Seahorse wasn't there. He was in the past. In fact, every session they ever had, hundreds upon hundreds of hours, focused on the past. It was all behind him. Brother Alan felt like a monkey. A monkey that had been staring at its own behind.

Everything's ready for the morning. The two men exit via the center aisle. Reverend Swit pauses by one of the chairs Brother Alan had meticulously placed, and cocks it.

[2]

"Todd! Sit up!"

"Gail?" His arm remains a blindfold. He just got home from school. He hasn't been on the couch two minutes.

"Up I said!"

He gets vertical, opens an eye. When she went off to veterinary school, she worried about his having to cope with Alan by himself. He was glad he didn't have to cope with her.

"Why are you even here?"

"I need you to tell me what in the goddamn hell is going on."

He knew this would happen. She got the same baloney about Alan's "business trip" and drove the two hours to interrogate him while Regina's at the senior center.

"He took a job with an evangelist."

"Be serious."

"I am."

"Doing what?"

"Being an example of how a man ends up in a hell of his own creation." Todd can't encapsulate it. He ends up telling her most of what he remembers from the letter.

"I don't like what I'm hearing. Does Harriet know about this?" Harriet is Alan's mother.

"No. Please don't call her."

"You're right." Gail hangs up. "I'm going over there."

Skip's dry cleaner hands him the letter. "This was in a pocket."

Skip had forgotten all about it. He'd found it on the floor outside the conference room. The salutation gave him the impression it was a personal note to Alan from his brother. He was planning to return it, and had nothing else to do, bored out of his skull, yet somehow it slipped his mind. Then suddenly Alan was gone. And he didn't even say goodbye.

Alan was Skip's dream boss. He let Skip leave early every Monday for his 4:30 appointment with his barber. Then of course there was the blunder for which Alan took full responsibility when he could've easily and understandably thrown Skip under the bus. The new guy is Alan's opposite, an incompetent coward who is intentionally unclear. Skip never knows whether to run to the barbershop or cancel.

The note as he unfolds it smells of banana. "I should've known something was wrong when I found this on the floor. Alan Fry never drops anything."

Mr. Fabiani is busy making sure all of Skip's

suits are on the rack. Skip reads the letter, then checks both sides again as if something's missing.

"I'm not sure what to make of this. Would you mind taking a look?"

"Me? I don't think so. It's our policy not to."

"I'm giving you permission. Here."

"I don't want it."

Mrs. Fabiani emerges from the back. "What's the problem?"

"He wants me to read a personal item."

She transfers the glasses from the top of her head to her face. "Give it to me."

Skip is happy having the brains of the operation on the case. He watches her expressions as she reads.

"Who is this Brother Alan?"

"He's my boss."

"And this reverend. He wants for the Brother Alan to be his—how do you say in English, *spettacolo da baraccone?*"

"Freak show," answers Mr. Fabiani.

"That's my concern," Skip tries to tell them. "It's not like him to go off and do something like this."

She gives it back. "Good luck."

[4]

Reverend Swit uses a Bible he took from the motel and replaced with Reverend Wilkinsen's, which was heavily scribbled in and falling apart. As Gerry Switzer, he had never touched a Bible. The closest he came was in a church during a funeral. It was in a rack on the back of the pew in front of him.

"Brother Alan, what does it mean to go forth and multiply?"

"Fornicate?"

"It's far less complicated than that. Go forth means leave the past behind. All you have is what's in front of you, which keeps changing. That means *you* have to keep changing. You can't keep being the same old you. That's what born again means. You multiply yourself, again and again and again."

The book claps shuts, heads bow. A big sigh comes from Brother Alan. What a relief not having to be Alan Fry anymore. He can be Brother Alan, or whoever. Identity crisis shmidenity crisis. Let Dr. Seahorse's seahorse put that in its pipe and smoke it.

[5]

The green juice Regina just blended up makes
Jasper wheeze. This is why fitness instructors are
discouraged from fraternizing with the members. In
the case of Jasper and Hank, however, there was no
stopping it. They started following her home every
Wednesday after Move & Grove. A year after Hank's
passing, it's still strange seeing Jasper without him.

"You need the Heimlich?"

"Maybe later," he says, pounding his chest.

She tries a sip. "Ich. Too much ginger. I don't
know even know what I'm doing anymore."

"You're missing your husband, that's what you're
doing."

"Who would expect?"

"Speaking of the Heimlich, did I ever tell you the
double Heimlich story?"

"Tell me again."

Jasper likes to change it up. This time he and
Hank are having lunch in a Chinese restaurant
(previously Italian). Jasper makes a funny remark
about the choking victim sign on the wall and Hank

24

inhales a chunk of sweet and sour pork. To which Jasper reacts by gagging on chow fun. It's three in the afternoon, they're the only customers, no staff in sight. They Heimlich one another, ending up on the floor coughing their brains out, and vomiting as well.

Regina isn't laughing. Would she miss Alan like Jasper misses Hank? She never thought about it before.

"Regina. You want him back? Let's go."

"Where? To find him?"

"No. To my urology appointment. Of course to find him. Where's the boy? Is he here?"

"He went somewhere on his bike. To his grandparents."

"Perfect. Have him stay there."

[6]

The doorbell rings. Usually Harriet gets it. When she decided to run off with Gail to find Alan, Abe was looking forward to the alone time. Then, when he saw the overnight bag, he got a little woozy.

"Simon, come in. I just made coffee."

Simon has never stepped foot inside before. Harriet wouldn't have it. He comes by only to get something blessed by Abe, who isn't even the rabbi anymore. Abe has blessed Simon's prune juice, cologne, tennis balls, stock portfolios, tires, wine glasses, sunglasses, dandruff shampoo, nose hair trimmer, plant food, slacks, brisket, brisket recipe, stamp collection, personal ads, lottery tickets, airline tickets, hernia belt, etc. When the new rabbi drew the line, Abe, to Harriet's disgust, agreed to continue blessing Simon's things. Last time it was a seashell candle for a lady friend. Today, a photograph. He follows Abe to the kitchen, peering around corners.

"Where's Harriet?"

"What is that, the picture of your mother again?"

26

"It's a new frame. The old one fell apart." Simon sits in Harriet's chair.

It's been a while since Abe brewed coffee. He's not allowed. One time he made it too strong even though he was 100% sure he had adhered to her exact measurements. This pot looks okay as far as he can tell. He fills the mugs, brings them to the table, sits, and holds his hands over the picture. After the little blessing, the hands fly to his face.

"Abe. She didn't pass, did she?"

"No."

"That's good to hear. You have skim?"

The hands tilt the head toward the fridge. "On the door."

Simon checks the expiration date, opens, sniffs. Abe hears him do all that and sit back down.

"Simon. I need your opinion about something."

"Hold on a second." He's drizzling in the milk and stirring at the same time. "This isn't decaf is it?"

"I don't know what she buys. Listen to me. My son is wandering around the boonies selling bibles."

"Adam?"

"Alan."

"Alan! That's right."

Abe peeks between fingers. Simon sips.

"Simon. I'm asking for your opinion."

"Is it just the Old Testament or both?"

"I don't want questions. I want to know what you think."

"What's to think? He's a grown man. He can do what he wants."

"That's what *I* said. Does anyone listen? No. They jump in the car."

The doorbell rings.

"Simon, do me a favor and go see who that is."

It took Abe half the night to get to sleep. And then when he woke up and Harriet wasn't there, he remembered she had left and went into a panic, afraid he'd never see her again.

"Look what the cat dragged in."

Abe lowers his hands to see who Simon is talking about.

"Todd! What is it? Where's your grandmother?"

"She went with Gail."

"I know that. Then what are you doing here?"

"I just stopped by."

"What for?"

"I don't know. To see how you're doing."

"How I'm *doing*? I'm fine. I'm not an invalid!"

"Don't yell at the boy," Simon tells him. "If you're

so worried about Harriet, let's go find her."

"Can we take your car?"

"Where's the Olds?"

"They took it."

"What's that piece of junk in the driveway?"

"That's Gail's."

"Okay then. My car it is." Simon's Monte Carlo is at the curb, about to be blessed by Abe once again.

[6]

The van slows to a crawl. Reverend Swit is looking past Brother Alan out the passenger's side window. Brother Alan looks as well. In the woods is a bear defecating copiously. Gail was right about the no pooping signs on the lawn: they *are* absurd. His confounded coprophobia deprived her of pets. No wonder she wants to be a vet. She gets to be around all the animals she wants.

The vehicle gathers speed. Brother Alan faces forward.

"You put me on hold for 20 minutes to come back and tell me there's nothing you can do?"

Both of Skip's ears are sore from the telephone. He's dying to scream at this blockhead but he's at work and has to keep his voice down.

"Sir. I'm going to say everything I've already said one more time, so please listen carefully. We have nothing to go on. We can't find anyone by the name of Gerald Swit or any establishment under the name Smackwater Motor Inn. You have failed to provide Mr. Fry's social security number, or any identifying information. All we have is a facsimile of a letter that contains no illegality or threat, a job offer which if Mr. Fry did accept does not constitute abduction."

"Let *me* say something one more time. This man *saved my ass*. The typographical error, *my* oversight, went out on 6,500 postcards. The premium had an *extra zero*. $300. Per month. For *dental* coverage. Please see the magnitude, sir. Had Mr. Fry not taken responsibility, I would be *finished*."

"Sir. As *I* have said. That story has no relevance and retelling it won't give it any. I'm going to provide you with two options, which you are free to regard or disregard, and then I'm going to have to end this call. Option #1: hire a private investigator."

"I'm hiring *you*. I'm paying 15% in federal tax every two weeks for *you* to investigate. That's what the 'I' in FBI stands for. Investigation."

"Option #2: Search for Mr. Fry via a search party or on your own."

PART THREE

[1]

"Nana, slow down." Gail can't steady the map with Harriet barreling through hairpin turns.

"You keep staring at that thing and it's not helping. Could you please reach up and turn this goddamn light off?" The Olds is a lot of car for Harriet to handle. The electric seat is all the way forward so she can reach the pedals and high as it'll go for visibility. The steering wheel is tilted down like in a bus, and she's been behind it all night. Gail can't be trusted to take over. That little garbage can she drives has dents galore.

A few miles back they passed a motel which unbeknownst to them and most people used to be called Smackwater Motor Inn. The name was changed after a drunken man shot his room to smithereens. The news report used a song about an outlaw called Smackwater and the motel became associated not with the melodious creek that lulls guests into a blissful slumber but with shotgun blasts. The owner got out the ladder and the letters and replaced SMACKWATER with MOUNTAIN. She wasn't about to order new writing pads when she had plenty of the old, which is what Reverend Gerald Swit wrote the letter on. Todd knew nothing of this when he told Gail the name of the motel. The only Smackwater she can find on the map is Smackwater Falls.

"Are we still on 29B?"

"Stop asking me that. We're just going. He has to be around here somewhere."

"It's raining, Nana. Why are you speeding up?"

"A few drops." The object swinging from the rearview clanks against the windshield, getting her attention for the first time. It's the old mezuzah with the traveler's prayer for a safe journey. Abe must have hung it there while she was packing. It had been around his mother's neck from Hungary to Ellis Island.

"Nana. Why are you stopping?"

"I didn't stop." Harriet's foot comes off the brake.

[2]

Brother Ray lies on a padded table with a hole for his face. He can see the sneakers of the people walking around bending and stretching everything. The cracked shin isn't their first concern. Brother Ray has diabetes, low blood pressure, cirrhosis, neuropathy, rheumatism, gout, psoriasis, apnea, fibromyalgia, bronchitis, arthritis, bursitis, and gingivitis. They have to keep moving his joints and circulating his blood or he'll be too stiff to walk when the leg heals. Breathing into the pain—this is what they keep telling him to do—feels like fanning embers embedded in his joints and organs.

Just as Brother Ray is about to pass out, a raven struts under the table. Reverend Swit gave a sermon about ravens. He said they never worry and he was right. This one hasn't a concern in the world.

[3]

Now it's Todd driving the Monte Carlo. He's six months from getting his permit, close enough for Simon who's exhausted in the back while Abe, who left his glasses at home, is the squinting co-pilot.

"Pass them already!"

Todd won't. He appreciates the taillights leading the way at night on a curvy road in a torrential downpour.

"Come on! They're going two miles an hour!"

"Let him drive. He's not killing anybody." Simon is looking at the picture of his mother. In the dark there's something in her smile he never saw before, a sad knowing that this face is replacing her real face. Nobody lives forever, Simey. This is the best I can do. Sorry, no more birthday cards from me.

The slowpoke pulls over. As they pass, Abe thinks he recognizes the car.

"Isn't that your mother?"

"Mine?" says Simon.

"Todd! What're you doing? Go back!"

[4]

"I just told you, sir, we *did* receive the fax. I've been looking at it since we've been on the phone. I still can't figure out from this letter what you expect us to report."

Skip has had it with her. He has to force himself to whisper. "A man. Has been. Abducted."

"So a missing person alert."

"Correct."

"We would need a photo."

"I don't have one right now."

"Do you have a sketch?"

Skip's jaw clenches. "No."

"Name of the investigating officer."

"There *isn't* one. I told you. Nobody will *do* anything."

"Sir, this is an actual news station, not the one on *Saturday Night Live*. We can't broadcast a crime without written permission from law enforcement."

"Listen to me. I don't have time to explain everything to you right now. I'm calling from work and I have a haircut appointment in less than 15 minutes. Hello? Are you there?"

"Good one! You had me going."

[5]

Rain from the night sky accompanies Bruno through the weeds that keep tweaking his few remaining whiskers. He no longer remembers the house he'd been sharing with five other cats, two dogs, and four humans including Gail who are earning outreach credits for rescuing animals and nursing them back to health. The screen slashed easily with the running start. The claw went right through followed by the rest of him.

He was a scrawny stray with gashes and scars the day he darted in front of Gail and led her down the sidewalk like a bodyguard who'd just fought off an attacker and resumed his position. At the stop sign she picked him up and carried him across the street. He hissed at a jogger, baring all five teeth, and a tough-guy name came to her.

"Easy, Bruno."

His claws retracted and she hasn't felt them since, only the pads, which are now supple from the Vitamin E. He was pressing them into her leg the other day hitting some nice meridian points while she gave him a talking-to about behaving in her absence. There was a quiver in her voice, and a smell of worry in her perspiration that lodged in his brain such that he's been unable to smell anything else, including the real smell. His spine keeps prickling with signals to find and protect her and he doesn't know where he's going.

6

"Regina," says Jasper. "Pardon me for interrupting, but you don't have your wipers on."

"I find them distracting."

"How can you possibly see?"

"Fine, if you're going to crap your pants about it." She sets them on intermittent. "Where was I?"

"The senior asks him to the prom."

"She asks *him*, a sophomore, and he says no!"

"Maybe he doesn't like her."

"We know the family! She's a nice girl! With a brain in her head! She got into Barnard early acceptance!"

"So what's his problem?"

She lowers her voice. "It's obvious. *She* would have to drive. The female driving the male."

"He was just driving a Monte Carlo."

"He doesn't have a license." She looks in the rearview. "Do you, Mr. Big Shot?"

Todd's pretending to be asleep. It has nothing to do with what Regina said. He doesn't want to go to a prom. Not hers. Not his. Not anyone's.

"You should go," says Jasper. "You don't have to marry her. Just go and have fun."

"He hates fun. He gets it from his father."

Todd rolls over and faces the upholstery.

7

The tent didn't weather last night's storm. It's now a shroud with a disaster underneath and lakes on top. Brother Alan goes and grabs an edge. "You're just going to stand there?"

Reverend Swit answers by doing just that. Maybe the muddy little man walking his ten-speed up the hill will help. He was in attendance at the previous township. He approached Brother Alan after the sermon, was about to say something, then walked away.

His heel keeps slipping off the kickstand. "Come on." Finally it lowers with a screech, followed by the firing of the van's engine. He watches Reverend Swit drive out of sight, then faces Brother Alan.

"Brother, man, there's something I need to tell you."

"He should be back soon."

"I can't talk to him. Not about this. You're not going to want to hear it but I have to tell somebody so I'm just going to go ahead and say it." He looks straight up. "I don't believe there's a God up there and I never did. I keep trying, but."

Brother Alan doesn't know what to say. What can you say about God? He was taught not to speak God's name and now he knows why. A name is a sound you have thoughts about, and none of them are real. They're all in your head.

The man keeps looking up, avoiding eye contact, when a wind whips through the wet trees, sending down big drops on his face. Slowly he lowers his gaze to Brother Alan until he's peering into eyes, and then right on through, like out a window and seeing the world for the first time.

"Wow."

With that, a branch that snapped last night and had been dangling by a strip of bark falls on Brother Alan's head.

[8]

The gentleman in 103 is in the bathroom with
the Bible from the nightstand. The lady, who just
told him they should live together, is on the phone
singing happy birthday to a grandson. She doesn't
look her age, but he does. Her plan was to take him
backpacking. When it stormed and she pulled into
the motel, he cried with relief and let her think it
was a wave of bittersweet disappointment.

The Bible is falling apart, nothing like the
new-smelling ones they typically have. He holds the
spine and jiggles the pages inside the thin leather
binding. He'd hate to hurt her feelings but he has his
artificial hip to consider, and the good one as well.
That romp in the night was like a nine car pile up.
He opens to a random verse for guidance:

> Consider what a great forest is set on fire by a small
> spark. The tongue also is a fire, a world of evil among the
> parts of the body. It corrupts the whole body, sets the
> whole course of one's life on fire, and is itself set on fire
> by hell. All kinds of animals, birds, reptiles and sea
> creatures are being tamed and have been tamed by
> mankind, but no human being can tame the tongue. It
> is a restless evil, full of deadly poison.

He doesn't know what this has to do with anything. What's he supposed to do, take a vow of silence? Never speak to her or anyone else again? Tempting, but is it realistic? Maybe what somebody wrote in the margin will shed some light:

> *Not just blabbing out loud,*
> *blabbing in your head.*

[9]

"Don't fill it so high!" Abe tells Skip. "You're killing our hands!"

Alan has found himself on a collapsed tent passing buckets of rainwater. There's a dent in his palm from the metal handle.

"I said don't want him exerting himself!" yells Harriet from the other end. "Did you not hear what Dane just told us? He took a branch on the head!"

"Whatever you say." Abe walks around Alan and hands the bucket to Todd who gives it to the reverend who empties it and tosses it back to Skip.

"Yow!" Jasper examines his calf. "He bit me!"

"Bruno!" Gail points. "What did we just talk about?"

Regina gives Alan a gentle rub on the head. "How's the noggin?" Something's different about her, but it's not her. It's him. He's seeing her. He's not thinking, just seeing.

"It's nice seeing you," he says.

"It's nice seeing *you*." She puts her hands on her

47

hips and pushes them forward. "Hey Simon, bend your knees! You're going to ruin your back!"

ALSO BY STEVE PRICE

Crab Apples: Stories & Poems
Back When Libraries Were Quiet
Music
An Orchid and A Man
Song of Scott
Marco J. Merola's Greatest Cries
A Key For Otis
Ruth Haikus
Elizabeth Hates Harvey
Brake Light
They Don't Have A Word For It
A Man In An Elevator
The Jungle Isn't Out There
Narcissus: The Man, The Myth, The Flower
John Doe's Diamond
Arrows of Love: A New Version of The Bhagavad Gita
A Bowler's View of the Tao Te Ching
Crawling Back To Patanjali
Assembly Instructions for Your Head
Writing From Scratch
How's Your Ice Cream?
White Elephant
Swami On Call
Coping With Bliss
Song of the Heart With No Walls
Clam In The Sky
Rocky (with Olive Price)
Can I Have One Moment of Peace?
Journal of Lovesickness, Vol. 11

To learn more, visit onemomentofpeace.org

9 7 9 8 3 5 7 7 2 1 3 0 3